My Sister the Sausage Roll

Barbara Ware Holmes

ILLUSTRATED BY
KAREN LEE SCHMIDT

D1211430

Hyperion Books for Children
New York

Printed in the United States of America.

First Edition
1 3 5 7 9 10 8 6 4 2

The artwork for each picture is prepared using pencils.
This book is set in 13-point Leawood Book.

Library of Congress Cataloging-in-Publication Data
Holmes, Barbara Ware.
My Sister the Sausage Roll / Barbara Ware Holmes ;
illustrated by Karen Lee Schmidt. — 1st ed.
p.   cm.
Summary: Although she does not like having a new baby sister, Eloise keeps an
eye on her while their father is away and finds herself learning to love her.
ISBN 0-7868-1182-X (pbk.) — ISBN 0-7868-2260-0 (lib. bdg.)
[1. Sisters—Fiction. 2. Babies—Fiction.] I. Schmidt, Karen Lee, ill. II. Title.
PZ7.H7337E1   1997
[Fic]—dc20   96-32512

For Cecil Odell Ware
—B. W. H.

1

Eloise Trombly examined her new baby sister. What she saw was a round red face, hair that stuck out straight in two places, and a dot on the side of her nose. What she heard and smelled she could not even *think* about.

"Ahh, I think she's cute," said Jenny, but Jenny was the kind of friend who tried to make you feel better, no matter what. "She's cuter than Chrissy's."

1

"Well, duh!" Chrissy's sister had had a rash all over her face that made her look sort of rotted.

"But not as good as Jason's."

They smiled at each other. "Jason's looks like Jason," Eloise pointed out. "I could live with a baby like that!"

Eloise looked in the crib again. "My mother calls this baby a 'leet-tle work of art.' Can you believe it?" She stuck a finger in her mouth and made a gagging sound. "I'd say more like a '*bee-eg*' sausage roll."

Jenny looked down at the baby. "She *is* like a sausage roll!" she said in surprise. Then she started laughing. She laughed and laughed. She laughed so hard that tears came into her eyes.

"Well, mothers have to love anything," she told Eloise, when she could finally talk. She sighed a happy sigh. "It's like a law or something. Plus, she probably figures she has to make up for your dad's not being here. You know—love her twice as much." Jenny knew a lot about how minds worked, since her mother was a psychologist. "It's what my mom does with me."

It *was*, Eloise thought. Jenny's father had left when she was a baby. Now her mother was like a slave, always running around trying to help Jenny not notice her father was missing.

"I guess." Though personally Eloise didn't see why her own mother had to work at it so hard. Mr. Trombly was only off working in a foreign country. He was definitely coming back.

After Jenny went home, Eloise wrote her father a letter:

Dear Dad,

Mary Alice is okay but mediocre. She looks like a sausage roll. Jenny and I give her a C. (Or an A as a sausage.)

You're not missing much.

Love,
Eloise

(She didn't want him feeling bad about not being around to see the baby. Who knew what kind of stuff her mother might be writing about her "leet-tle work of art"?)

Her father wrote right back (which meant the letter came two weeks later):

Dear Eloise,

I'm sorry to hear the baby is only a C, but I'm sure with you as a big sister and fine example she'll improve with age, as does fine wine and cheese. (I'm not so sure about sausage.) Most of us start out as only Cs (or even lower!). I myself was

4

a D. I'm counting on you to be there for both your mother and sister.

Love,
Dad

P.S. Say hello to Jenny.

"How would you grade me when I was a baby?" Eloise asked her mother. She asked from across the room. Mrs. Trombly was changing the baby's diaper.

Her mother looked up in surprise. "How would I *grade* you?"

"Right. Like was I an A, a B, or a C?"

"Oh. Well, let me see. I'd say you were an A in everything except for maybe temper. In temper you were a C minus, minus, minus."

"Um-hmm. Well then how would you grade Mary Alice?"

Her mother pressed her nose to the baby's. "How would I grade my little pumpkin?" she asked in baby talk. "I'd give her a C in diaper rash, a B in eating, and an A in everything else."

Eloise gave her mother a D- in grading.

"And I'd give her an A+ for making it here in the first place with such a creaky old mother. She's like a miracle baby."

Like a miracle baby? Eloise hurried to her room to write her father:

Dear Dad,

I'll do my best with Mary Alice. Just don't tell me I have to touch her. And yes, I AM there for her, and she's THERE for me, too—her crib is in my bedroom taking up all the space. You were not a D. Jenny says you made that up so Mary Alice wouldn't sound like such a loser. Pretty nice of you.

Love,
Eloise

P.S. Whatever Mom is telling you is probably not true.

2

The next day, when Eloise and Jenny came in from school, Mrs. Trombly had Mary Alice dressed in clothes that had laces and ruffles and shiny buttons. Jenny and Eloise looked at each other.

"Did you ever do that to me?" Eloise asked her mother.

Her mother smiled. "Are you hoping that I'll say no?"

"YES!"

"No," her mother answered. "I never did this to you."

Jenny ran her hand across her forehead, wiping off make-believe sweat. "Whew!" she said.

The doorbell rang. "Oh, there's the photographer!" Mrs. Trombly lifted the baby out of the crib and wrapped her snugly in a blanket. "Hold her a minute," she said, handing the bundled-up lump to Eloise. "Don't let her spit up on her dress."

Eloise frowned down at the lump. It was going to spit up?

"Can you believe it?" Jenny said. "She's having her *picture taken* like this!"

"Yurgle," the baby said, her head wobbling back and forth. Her eyes seemed to be looking at Eloise, though with new babies Eloise knew you could never tell for sure. A wobbly neck might just have bounced the eyes in your direction. The eyes were sort of nice, Eloise

noticed. They were the color of her father's.

Mrs. Trombly came into the room, followed by a man with a camera. He stood too close and peered down at Mary Alice. "Well, well, well!" he boomed. "What have we here?"

"What we have here is a *bee-eg* sausage roll," said Eloise under her breath, but then she felt a burst of pity. She could feel Mary Alice stiffen and start to squirm. She was hot inside the blanket and she couldn't kick her feet, and now this stranger with the loud voice was going to take an obnoxious picture of her in a silly dress.

"Babies are like—totally helpless," she said to Jenny while they watched the photographer take the pictures. She could feel the anger stirring inside her at the injustice of it. "I bet I hated being a baby."

Jenny smiled at her. "Yep," she said. "I bet you did."

"Is this what you're sending to Dad?" Eloise asked when she saw the finished picture. Mary Alice looked like one of those dolls with a rubber head you wouldn't buy in a million years.

"Yes, it is."

Dear Dad,
    Mom is sending a picture of Mary Alice that is not even close to real. Try and ignore it and keep it out of your wallet. I ask this for Mary Alice.
Love,
Eloise
P.S. The baby has your eyes. It's the only nice thing about her. Why don't you come home and see them?

Her father wrote back:

Dear Eloise,
    I received your mother's picture of Mary Alice and I see what you mean. No baby could look like this and live. I have a

suggestion. Borrow your mother's camera and take me some honest shots. I'm sure Jenny could help direct. Thanks. I'd give a million bucks and my favorite shirt (which I'm wearing right now) if I could come home and stay there. I miss you so much my stomach flips when I think of your pretty face. Unfortunately, when you work for the government, you can't always call the shots. Just keep remembering how much I love you.

Love,
Dad

"Wow," Jenny said when she read the letter. "His stomach flips. That is just the most beautiful thing a dad can say to his daughter." She looked sad for a minute, then she brightened as fast as she'd slumped. "He wants me to help direct! We'd better not tell your mother, or she'll take over. You know your mother."

Oh yes, Eloise knew her mother. They made plans for Saturday, when Mrs. Trombly would be napping.

"Call me the minute she's sleeping," Jenny told her.

On Saturday, Eloise tiptoed into the living room and looked in her mother's desk. She found the camera. Did it have any film? she wondered. She held it as far out in front of herself as she could, with it facing in, and smiled and clicked. The flash exploded and the film moved forward. Yep. Film was in it, but she was now blinded for life. She dialed Jenny's number with her eyes closed to see if she could do it.

"Franco's Pizza!"

Eloise hung up and dialed again, this time keeping her eyes open. "I found the camera," she whispered to Jenny. "And my mom's taking a nap. Come right now."

In the bedroom, they each stood on a chair and looked down at Mary Alice, who was fast asleep. Eloise took a picture of Jenny looking.

"Sleeping would be a good shot," Jenny whispered. "Babies really do sleep." Eloise clicked and the flash went off. Mary Alice opened her eyes and looked up.

"Smile," said Jenny, and Mary Alice did, until the flash went off again. Then she began to scream.

"Keep on going," Jenny ordered. "Babies really do scream. They really do turn purple." Eloise went on clicking.

"Eloise? What on earth . . . ?" It was her mother. Eloise took her picture as she rushed through the door.

"Dad asked me to take some pictures," she explained. "Real ones, not the kind that that man took."

Her mother's eyebrows went up. Eloise took a picture of that.

"Oh. Well, that's very nice, Eloise. But why don't I hold Mary Alice while you do it?" She picked the baby up and jiggled her until she

was quiet. "There. *Now* take the baby's picture." Mary Alice looked sort of surprised, as if the feelings had been jiggled out of her and she wondered where they had gone. Eloise didn't dare look at Jenny or say what she was thinking. She just took the picture.

When the pictures came back, there was one great close-up of Eloise's face from the nose down and a cool picture of Jenny, looking ready to attack.

The baby looked crooked and upside down in all of her pictures, and in one she had no head, but at least she looked like a person instead of a doll.

There was also a picture of Mrs. Trombly rushing in frowning, a picture of her eyebrows, and one of a blank-looking baby with mother that was boring beyond belief. These were all pretty real.

"These pictures are great, Eloise," her

mother said. "This is just how Mary Alice looks when you lean over her crib. Daddy will love seeing that." And she put them all in an envelope and addressed it to John Trombly.

Her father wrote as soon as he got them:

Dear Eloise,

I love your pictures! Now *these* are what I call real-life shots. Please thank Jenny for her excellent directing. It's hard for a father to be away from his children when he knows how quickly they're changing. I need you to be my eyes and ears with Mary Alice. When you write me letters and send your pictures I learn about both of you. I could use some more pictures of you, though. Maybe one from the nostrils up and one of the whole caboodle.

Love always,
Dad

"Do I have a caboodle?" Eloise asked her mother.

"Beats me!" her mother said.

3

It's sad when you think about it," Jenny said, after she read Mr. Trombly's letter. "The man has never seen his own daughter. Everyone wants to see his own daughter, even if it is only Mary Alice."

"You're probably right," sighed Eloise. It was going to be work, being her father's eyes and ears. It would mean having to look at the baby on purpose.

"And think about *this*—Mary Alice doesn't know her father! Now that's *really* sad."

Right again. Eloise looked into the crib where Mary Alice was waking up. She did look kind of lonely and fatherless. Her father's eyes weren't happy about that.

"I know!" said Jenny. "Why don't we show her his picture and tell her some stuff about him?"

Eloise considered the idea. It seemed pretty dumb. "Mary Alice is just a baby," she pointed out. "She's not going to know what we're saying."

Jenny frowned. "How do you know that? You can't tell what a baby is thinking. She might understand every word we say."

They looked in at Mary Alice who looked right back, as if she *had* understood every word.

Jenny picked up the framed photograph of Mr. Trombly that Eloise kept by her bed and carried it to the crib. "Look, Mary Alice," she said. "This is your dad."

Mary Alice looked. She gurgled at the picture.

"He is a very cool person. A wonderful dad and husband. He's made your mother completely happy."

"Not completely happy," Eloise pointed out. "He goes away a lot."

Jenny ignored her. "For example," she went on. "He almost never gets mad. Unless, of course, you do something really stupid, like scratch your initials on the side of his two-hundred-dollar briefcase." She shot Eloise a look.

Eloise shot the look back. "I was only a kid," she said.

"And he has this great sense of humor," Jenny continued. "He loves playing jokes. One time . . ."

Eloise sighed and stopped listening. This could go on for hours. It usually did when the subject was Mr. Trombly. Jenny had been in love with him since the minute she was born. Eloise peeked in at Mary Alice, who looked sort of hypnotized.

That night, Eloise wrote to her father:

Dear Dad,

Being your eyes and ears will not be easy, but I'm giving it a try. The first thing I have to tell you is that somehow, when I wasn't looking, Mary Alice lost the dot on the side of her nose. This has improved her appearance. Also, her hair has grown into curls that are fairly nice. She's now a B-. (Or a C as a sausage roll.) That's all I have to report.

        Love,

        Your Eyes and Ears,

        Eloise

She didn't tell him about their plan to teach Mary Alice about him. It might not work. In brains, Mary Alice could be a D–. Or even worse!

Before she went to bed, she carried the picture to the crib. "Look," she whispered. "This is serious. This is our dad. Say, 'Hi, Daddy.'" Of course Mary Alice couldn't talk yet, but she looked as if she'd *like* to say it. She looked as if she *thought* it.

Eloise was fairly impressed. She had an idea. What if she showed Mary Alice this picture every day and night until she *did* learn to talk? Until she *could* say, "Hi, Daddy"? One day, her father would come home and walk up to that crib. He'd look in. He'd smile. Mary Alice would smile back. Then she'd say, "Hi, Daddy." Their father would not believe his ears. "She knows me!" he'd say, then ask Mrs. Trombly how such a miracle could

happen. Eloise's mother wouldn't know, of course, because she wouldn't be the one who'd had the idea or done any of the work.

"Jenny and I thought a baby should know her father," Eloise would explain. "So we showed her your picture and told her all about you. And I taught her to say, 'Hi, Daddy.'"

Her father would be amazed. "Incredible!" he'd say. "Brilliant! Imagine that!" Her mother's mouth would be open but no words would come out.

"Memorize this picture," she told Mary Alice. "And learn to talk. One of these days we're going to make our daddy a very happy man."

4

Eloise worked hard at being the eyes and ears for her father. She noticed every new thing that Mary Alice did. The first time the baby rolled over, Eloise wrote her father all of the boring details. And when Mary Alice sat up, Eloise was there to record it. Sometimes she put a joke in her letters, such as "now Mary Alice can roll over, sit up, and play dead." (These were the things Jenny's dog did.)

Her father liked that one. He wrote back:

Dear Eloise-Eyes-and-Ears,
　　I always wanted a daughter who could do tricks. Perhaps we can train Mary Alice to balance a ball on her nose when she gets a little older. What do you think?
　　　　　　　　　　Love,
　　　　　　　　　　Dad

"Hey!" Jenny said when she read the letter. "If he wants a daughter who can do tricks, he could have me. I can balance a ball on my nose!"

"Plus, you'd come whenever he called you," Eloise added. "And fetch him his slippers!"

"I would. Hey, his slippers! We should show Mary Alice his slippers!"

While Mrs. Trombly was in the kitchen, they tiptoed into her bedroom and came back with the slippers.

"Look, Mary Alice!" Jenny said, holding

them over the crib. "Here's what your dad likes to wear on his feet when he's home just relaxing. Aren't they the grossest?" Jenny and Eloise agreed it was amazing to have your feet be across an ocean and their smell still be in your slippers.

Mary Alice wrinkled her nose in appreciation.

Jenny came every day and told Mary Alice at least one new thing about Mr. Trombly. Sometimes she told stories and sometimes she told facts, such as "Your daddy hates asparagus. He calls it asparagusting." If she ran out of ideas for things to tell, she'd sneak into his closet and bring back a piece of clothing.

And every night and every morning, Eloise held the picture over Mary Alice's crib and said, "Say, 'Hi, Daddy.'" Every day Mary Alice looked a little happier to see it. She wriggled and smiled and got up to touch the picture. But she didn't say, "Hi, Daddy."

Fall became winter. Mr. Trombly did not come home. He wasn't there for Christmas or for Eloise's birthday.

One day, when Mrs. Trombly was reading a letter from her husband, she gasped in surprise. "Geez Louise, Eloise!" she said. "Your father's growing a mustache."

Eloise looked up from the book she was reading. A mustache? How much did a mustache change how somebody looked? "No hair on the chin, right?" she asked her mother.

"Well he *says* just a mustache. Isn't that enough?"

That night, Eloise drew a line on the glass of the picture, under her father's nose. When Mary Alice saw it, she paused before she wiggled.

"This is how Daddy looks now," Eloise told her. "Say, 'Night-night, Daddy.'" Mary Alice pulled herself up and touched the glass of the picture, but she didn't speak.

"Jeepers," Jenny said the next day. "Your father with a mustache!" She stared at the picture for a very long time. "Well," she said finally. "It does make him look sort of younger."

"But he's not," Eloise said. "He's getting older. And changing."

Jenny had nothing to say to this.

The minute Jenny went home, Eloise wrote to her father:

Dear Daddy,

   Mary Alice's fuzz has turned into a curl that looks like a question mark. The question is, WHERE IS MY DADDY?? (*And when is he coming home?* Eloise wanted to add, but didn't.)

                    I love you and miss you,
                    Eloise

Two weeks later, the answer came from her father. It said:

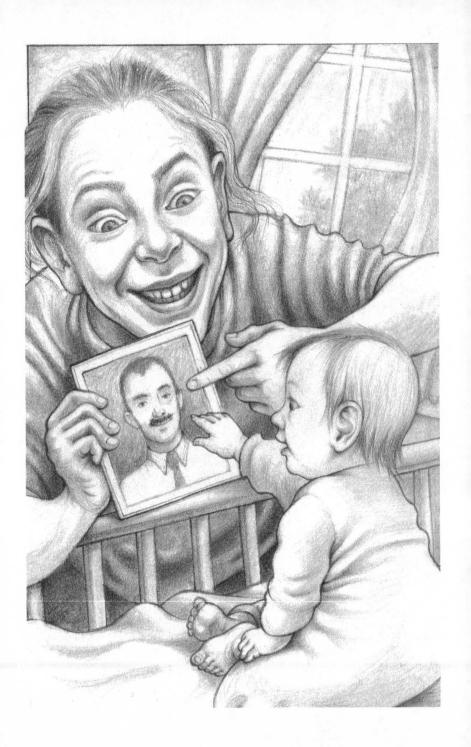

Dear Eloise,

I HAVE A CHILD WITH A QUESTION MARK ON HER HEAD? That's the saddest thing I've ever heard! The minute I read those words, I wanted to hop on a plane with a pair of scissors and cut that curl off. I hope you've told her a *little* about her father—you know, how he looks like a movie star and sings like Pavarotti. It will be a while yet before I can be there to be a real father. I'm more sorry than you can know.

I LOVE YOU, TOO,
Daddy

Jenny smiled when she read the letter. "Oh, I think we've told Mary Alice a *little* about her father!" she said.

Eloise didn't answer. *Hearing* about a father wasn't at all the same as having one living with you, and Jenny knew it, too.

5

Outside the world kept changing as winter turned into springtime. Mary Alice was changing, too. She could say "Ma-ma" and "bye-bye" and "Denny" for "Jenny." But she would not say, "Hi, Daddy." Or anything *close* to Eloise. Not that Eloise cared, of course.

One day, Eloise and Jenny took her to the park in her stroller to feed the ducks and geese.

"Your daddy likes ducks," Jenny said. "He has them on two of his shirts."

By the time they came home, Mary Alice could say *"honk"* and *"quack-quack."*

"'Da-da' is a lot easier than *'quack-quack,'*" Eloise told her. "You're just being mean to Jenny and Eloise." She held up the picture. "Now say, 'Hi, Daddy.'"

Mary Alice smiled. *"Quack-quack,"* she replied.

"You sure have a stubborn streak," Jenny told her.

"Tweak!" said Mary Alice.

Jenny and Eloise looked at each other and sighed.

"Let's try something different," Jenny suggested. "Stop saying you-know-what when you show her the picture. She'll be so used to hearing it maybe she'll say it for herself."

That night when Eloise held the picture up

over the crib she didn't say a word. Mary Alice wiggled and smiled and tried to touch it, but she didn't say, "Hi, Daddy." She didn't look as if she even noticed the words were missing.

Eloise tried again the next morning. Again, Mary Alice looked happy just touching the picture.

"Okay, then," Jenny said when Eloise told her. "How about this—you say, 'Don't you *dare* say, "Hi, Daddy"! Do *not* say it! No, no, no!' She'll do it because you don't want her to. That used to work with me when I was a stubborn baby. For a while my mom had to tell me to do exactly the opposite of whatever she really wanted, and it always worked. It's called reverse psychology. My mom says if she'd used it on my father, they might still be married."

It sounded pretty weird to Eloise, but she guessed it was worth a try.

"Don't you *dare* say, 'Hi, Daddy'!" she told

Mary Alice that night. "I mean it! Do NOT say, 'Hi, Daddy.' No, no, no! And *never* say 'Eloise'!"

Mary Alice looked at her. "No, no, no!" she repeated.

"You are the world's most annoying baby," Eloise said, feeling a tiny bit of respect for a baby who could be this stubborn.

"That's all right," Jenny said when she heard the news. "I have a better idea. Here's what you do: you sit on the floor beside her bed and whisper 'Hi, Daddy' over and over while she's asleep. That's how my mom learns French, but she does it with a tape recorder. It fixes the message in your brain when you don't even know you're listening."

Eloise sighed. This was getting to be very hard work. Good thing her father was worth it—Mary Alice wasn't.

That afternoon, while Mary Alice was

napping, Eloise sat on the floor beside the crib. "Hi, Daddy. Hi, Daddy. Hi, Daddy," she said, over and over again, but the only thing that happened was that she fell asleep and woke up with lines on her cheek.

After dinner, Mary Alice took her first steps. Luckily, Eloise-Eyes-and-Ears was there to see it.

Dear Dad,

The sausage roll walks! Tonight Mary Alice took her first real steps. She was standing by Mom's feet, hanging on to the coffee table, when she saw her bear across the room and wanted it. She took two wobbling steps, then crashed. It was a B-. (Or maybe an A for effort. But don't feel bad about missing it. It wasn't that exciting.)

Love,
Eloise

Writing this letter made Eloise feel sad. It *had* been exciting, though Eloise would never say so out loud.

"Couldn't Dad get one little weekend off to pop in for a visit?" she asked her mother. Of course, she already knew the answer.

Her mother looked so unhappy that Eloise was sorry she'd brought it up. "Nice idea, but no cee-gar," her mother said, sighing. "Your father's job is top secret and very, very important. Nobody else can do it. But he'll be home before long. Or so one supposes."

The next morning, Eloise watched her mother put her father's eyeglasses into a box and address it to John Trombly. "Daddy says his eyes are bothering him from having to read so much. He wants to go back to wearing his glasses instead of his contact lenses."

That night Eloise drew two circles on the glass of the photograph and showed it to

Mary Alice. "This is how Daddy looks now," she told her. "In case you care. Would you please say, 'Hi, Daddy!'? Would you please say, 'Thank you for informing me of this, sister Eloise'?"

Mary Alice touched one of the circles. "Gwasses," she said. Then she laid down and went to sleep, looking very happy.

Eloise stared at the picture of her father for a very long time before she fell asleep. Looking at how he was changing.

6

I give up," Eloise told Jenny. They were outside on the playground at school. "This baby is making me crazy."

"You *are* acting sort of weird," Jenny agreed.

"I am? Like how?"

Jenny looked thoughtful. "Like just now, in the cafeteria when Jason offered you part of his sandwich—a part that his *lips* had touched!—you said, 'No, thank you.'"

"I *did*?" Eloise stared at Jenny. She couldn't remember lunchtime. She couldn't remember Jason. She *was* going crazy!

After school, she hurried home to write to her father:

Dear Dad,

Mary Alice is turning into your sort of normal B baby, while I'm turning into a totally crazy person. This makes me worried and upset, which will probably make me crazier. What do you think I should do?

Love,
Eloise

She knew one thing that she would do.

"I'll stop worrying about *you*," she told Mary Alice, who ignored her and went on playing. That night, the baby didn't even seem to notice when Eloise didn't show her the photograph.

Mr. Trombly's answer came several weeks later. By now spring had become the summer, and school was almost over.

Dear Eloise,
 Relax. Going crazy is a normal part of the aging process. I look forward to meeting this crazy new you, because guess what? I'm coming home soon!! I'll write your mother the details. Oh, Eloise, isn't life wonderful? Or at least it will be soon!
 I love you, sweetheart,
 Daddy

"Oh, hallelujah!" shouted Mrs. Trombly. She and Eloise and Mary Alice danced around the living room until the baby's feet got tangled and they tripped over her and they all laid on the floor, laughing and laughing.

* * *

Mr. Trombly was coming home "sometime in the evening or night" of July 2. Jenny and Eloise worked all day helping Mrs. Trombly get the house ready. They hung streamers and balloons and a big sign that said **WELCOME HOME, MYSTERY MAN!** The "Mystery Man" part was Jenny's idea. She pointed out that no one really knew what Mr. Trombly looked like these days now that he had his mustache and glasses, and maybe other new things, too.

When they were done, Jenny and Eloise sat down and waited. Eloise had a knot where there used to be a stomach.

"But 'sometime in the evening or night' could mean anytime," Mrs. Trombly said when she saw them. "Midnight. Maybe later. Mystery Men don't come when you think they should."

Jenny and Eloise looked at each other. "Then I'm spending the night," said Jenny.

Mrs. Trombly brought the roll-away cot into Eloise's room and opened it up in the corner. "Well this will be nice," she said. "All his little chickens in one basket."

"Cluck," said Jenny.

When the bed was ready, Mrs. Trombly gave Eloise and Jenny permission to wait up until midnight. Mary Alice, however, had to go to bed at once. "This is one little chicken that will have to meet her daddy tomorrow," she said. "Now you girls get ready for bed and come on out here."

"I *am* ready for bed," said Jenny, who was planning on sleeping in her new plaid shorts and her huge turquoise T-shirt. Mr. Trombly had once said it made her eyes look deep and mysterious. Eloise thought it made her look like a camping tent, but she didn't want to tell her.

When Mrs. Trombly left the room, both of them stared into the crib. "This is your last chance, Mary Alice," said Eloise. She held the picture up. "Say, 'Hi, Daddy. Hi, Daddy. Hi, Daddy'!"

Mary Alice smiled at the picture. She talked to it in the language she sometimes used that nobody understood, throwing in a few words like "gwasses" and "tweak" and "no, no, no." But she wouldn't say, "Hi, Daddy"!

"You are a hard case to crack," Jenny told her.

"She's a pain," said Eloise. "And maybe also a genius."

By eleven o'clock, there was still no Mr. Trombly. At midnight, Eloise's mother made them go to bed.

"Fine," said Eloise. "But I'm not going to sleep."

"Me neither," promised Jenny.

"You wake that baby and you're in mighty big trouble," Mrs. Trombly told them. "And stay in your separate beds."

"She can make me lie here," whispered Jenny. "And she can make me not talk. But she can't make me not listen!"

"Me neither!" said Eloise.

And so they listened. They heard cars going by. Voices talking in the street. Car doors opening and shutting. But no Mr. Trombly. They listened and listened.

"I'm wrinkling my shirt," Jenny said much later, but the words sounded kind of funny and slurred and Eloise thought that she might be saying them in her sleep.

"Um," Eloise answered. "Feeple moo."

7

Eloise was dreaming about her father. At first he was wearing glasses and riding in a car, but then he was on a horse and the horse was galloping hard. Her father was wearing a cowboy hat and he was looking for Eloise everywhere he went, calling out her name. "Eloise-se, Eloise-se." He said it softly. "Wake up, I'm finally home." Eloise wanted to wake up and see her father, but she couldn't do it, even with the light shining around her. Her

eyes were too heavy with sleeping and dreaming. Now her father was also wearing a mustache and when he took off his hat his hair was all wavy and long—not at all like his own—and the horse was galloping harder and taking him out of sight.

"Eloise! Wake up, please. Show me those beautiful eyes of yours." Eloise smiled. She opened her eyes and saw her father's face. His regular face, without his glasses or mustache or cowboy hat. His hair was still short and curly.

"There they are!" her father said happily. "Still as blue and beautiful as ever, even after the work I've put them through!"

Eloise stared. It *was* her father! Her *real* father, and not the one in the dreams. She sat up and looked closer.

"Dad?" Her father smiled and nodded. Eloise hugged him. She thought she couldn't hug him long enough if she hugged for a million years.

"Man, have I missed you," he said softly. "My favorite crazy oldest daughter."

"I've missed you, too."

"Hey, wow!" Jenny sat up on the cot. "I thought that I was dreaming, but it's really you!" She leaped off her bed and onto Eloise's.

Mr. Trombly laughed. "The Mystery Man returns. How're you doing, sweetheart?" He gave Jenny a hug. "I'm really glad you're here. I've missed you, too."

Jenny beamed. "And I've missed you. But hey, you don't have a mustache or glasses!"

Mr. Trombly patted at his pocket. "The glasses are here, but the mustache is history. We Mystery Men have to keep our women guessing. And now," he said, "where is this Mystery Daughter?"

"Out like a light," said Mrs. Trombly, who was standing beside the crib, smiling and waiting. "Snoring like her father."

They all crossed the room and stared down at Mary Alice, who'd slept soundly through the noise. She really was snoring like her father! Eloise wondered how she'd been able to stand sleeping with her all this time.

Mr. Trombly whistled softly. "Oh my, what a beauty," he said. "And will you look at how big she's gotten, without one bit of help from a father." He sounded sad. Eloise thought how much he would have loved his surprise, if only it had worked.

At that moment Mary Alice opened her eyes and looked up. She looked right at her father. She smiled. She wiggled and bounced.

"Well, look at this," Mr. Trombly said, excited. "I think she's glad to see me! I think she somehow knows me." He reached into the crib and started to lift her up, but suddenly Mary Alice grew stiff. A wild look came into her eyes.

"No!" she hollered. "No, no, no!" She kicked and screamed. Eloise had never heard her scream so loudly. Her feet beat at her father's shirt.

"Why, Mary Alice!" said Mrs. Trombly. She reached out and took the baby and tried to hold her still. "Sh-h-h! Mary Alice, it's only your own daddy!" But Mary Alice was in a panic. She kicked and screamed and buried her face in her mother's shoulder.

Mr. Trombly looked very disappointed. "She seemed so glad to see me. What did I do wrong?"

Eloise knew at once. Mary Alice had thought he was the picture, and a picture didn't pick you up!

Eloise rushed across the room and grabbed her father's picture. "Look, Mary Alice," she said, holding it up to the baby's face. "*This* is the picture. See? Mary Alice, look!"

Mary Alice did look. She hiccuped and

stopped crying. She reached out and touched the picture, then stuck a thumb in her mouth.

"This is the picture, and *that's* our daddy." Mary Alice looked cautiously at Mr. Trombly then back at the picture. She laid her head on her mother's shoulder and hiccuped again.

Mr. Trombly was clearly puzzled.

"We've been showing her your picture," Jenny explained. "And telling her all about you. We told her at least one thing every day."

"But then she thought you were the picture instead of the person," Eloise added. "We never thought of that."

"You mean I scared her because I moved?" Mr. Trombly looked relieved and then sympathetic. "Well, poor little thing." His voice grew quiet. "How about this then," he said. "I'll sit here in this chair and won't touch her until she's ready." He sat down in Mrs. Trombly's rocker but didn't let it rock. "Not moving is something I used to be very good at. I majored in it at school."

Mary Alice narrowed her eyes and stared at her father, clearly thinking things over.

"See, Mary Alice?" Eloise said. "This is the man Jenny told you about. The one who's perfect, except for his stinky feet."

Mr. Trombly frowned. "Jenny thinks I have stinky feet?"

Jenny pulled her T-shirt up high enough for her head to slide inside it. She really *did* look like a tent.

"But that's the only bad thing Jenny told her," Eloise hurried on. "While she was giving her all of the facts. We wanted Mary Alice to know her real father."

"Well, that *is* one of the facts," Mr. Trombly agreed. "Man, how did I get so lucky? You girls are the best." Jenny's head popped out of the shirt again.

"They're also a little surprising," said Mrs. Trombly.

"I've been trying to teach her to say, 'Hi, Daddy,'" Eloise told him. "She wouldn't do it, though. She has this amazing stubborn streak."

"Tweak!" Mary Alice shouted, then stuck her finger back in her mouth.

Everyone laughed.

"She won't say 'Eloise' either," Eloise added.

Her father smiled. "I suppose she'll say them both when she's good and ready. I can outwait a stubborn streak. I can outwait anything. Someday she'll be a joy to me, like her big sister and her big sister's friend have been. I admire all of my strong-minded women."

Mary Alice pulled her thumb out of her mouth and hiccuped again. She looked at her father. She looked for a long, long time. Then she smiled.

"Hi, Eloise!" she bellowed.

Say Cheese!

We're sure you'll have a big smile on your face when you do these puzzles!

"C" Is for Average

At first, Eloise gave her baby sister a grade of C. In the picture below, there are several items that begin with the letter C. Find and circle all the things that start with C.

Mail Call

Eloise wrote lots of letters to her dad while he was away on business. And Eloise's dad wrote lots of letters to her. Connect the dots by twos to find a place Eloise went to often.

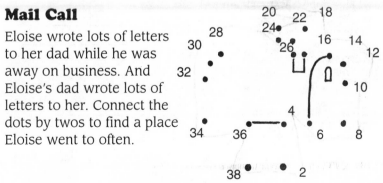

57

The Loaded Camera

Eloise and Jenny were excited to take some candid photos of baby Mary Alice. Eloise searched her home for a camera with film in it. Can you find the camera below with film? The camera that's different from the rest has film in it.

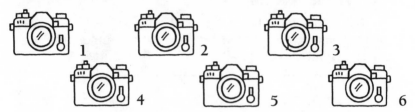

Look and Listen

While Mr. Trombly was away, he asked Eloise to be his eyes. Read the clues and use your answers to fill in this crossword puzzle. Here's a hint: All the answers have to do with seeing or hearing.

Down
1. This part of your body helps you to see and hear and it rhymes with "train."

2. You do this with your eyes and it rhymes with "tree."

3. This lights up the sky in red, orange, yellow, green, blue, indigo, and violet.

Across
4. This can't be seen and rhymes with "round."

5. There are five senses: touch, sight, smell, taste, and _____.

All in the Family

The Tromblys have many family photos in their home. Can you tell which of the photos is of Eloise's great-great-uncle on her father's side? Follow the clues to find out.

Clues:

1. He's wearing glasses.
2. His shirt is solid.
3. He doesn't have a beard.
4. He's wearing a hat.
5. His hat has a feather in it.

An Amazing Maze

When a letter from Mr. Trombly arrived saying that he would be coming home soon, everyone was ecstatic! Help bring Mr. Trombly back to his family. Follow the maze and get him home safely.

Puzzle Answers

"C" Is for Average

Look and Listen

Mail Call

An Amazing Maze

The Loaded Camera
Camera #2 is different

All in the Family
#4 is Eloise's uncle